When the Cousins Came

Katie Yamasaki

HOLIDAY HOUSE 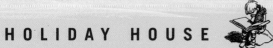 NEW YORK

FOR ALL THE COUSINS WITH LOVE:
Breandain, Chris, Cynthia, Heather, Jenny, Jesse,
Jessica, Little Jimmy, Kate, Margaret, Marie, Mariko,
Mark, Big Matt, Little Matt, Moi, Naomi, Natalie,
Nate, Norm, Patrick, Seth, Shantih, Siobhan,
Sylvia, and Takei.

Copyright © 2018 Katie Yamasaki
All Rights Reserved
HOLIDAY HOUSE is registered in the U.S. Patent and Trademark Office.
Printed and bound in November 2017 at Hong Kong Graphics and Printing Ltd., China.
The artwork was created with mixed media collage: acrylic paint, gouache paint, pastel,
colored pencil and hand-painted cut paper.
www.holidayhouse.com
First Edition
1 3 5 7 9 10 8 6 4 2
Library of Congress Cataloging-in-Publication Data

Yamasaki, Katie, author, illustrator.
When the cousins came / Katie Yamasaki. — First edition.
pages cm
Summary: Even though Lila's cousins do some things differently, Lila loves
when they come to visit.
ISBN 978-0-8234-3457-2 (hardcover)
[1. Cousins—Fiction. 2. Japanese Americans—Fiction.] I. Title
PZ7.Y19157Wh 2016
[E]—dc23
2014048569

The night before the cousins came, I couldn't sleep.
I couldn't wait to paint together, ride bikes together and
camp outside together.

My brother, Koji, was a baby, but my cousins were big
kids like me. "Finally, someone to play with!" I thought.

When the cousins came, Rosie had her hair in two puffy balls on top of her head. My hair was in two flat braids that pointed straight down. Takeo's hair was like a little shark fin.

"Four boys in my class have Mohawks," said Takeo.

"Oh," I said. Nobody in my class had a Mohawk.

Rosie and Takeo helped me make
my hair look like a little shark fin too.

When the cousins came, I invited them to ride bikes.
"We brought our own wheels," said Rosie.

Takeo and Rosie sped off on their skateboards,
and I chased after them on my bike.

Later, Rosie helped me balance on the board.

I helped Takeo balance on the bike.

When it was dinnertime, we had noodles.
Rosie asked for chopsticks.
"Here you go!" said Mom.
"We have chopsticks?" I asked.
"Hold them like this," said Takeo.

I tried . . .

and tried.

After dinner I asked the cousins if they wanted to go for a night walk.

"Night is scary," said Rosie.

"We don't go outside at night," said Takeo. "Something might get you."

"It's okay," I said. "I promise."

As we walked outside, Rosie and
Takeo held hands tightly. I wished they
would hold my hands too.

Fireflies glowed brightly, slowly turning
their lightbulb bodies on and off.
    "What is that?!?" asked Takeo. I caught a firefly
and cupped it in my hands. The firefly bumped gently
against the walls of my palms.
    "Just look," I whispered to Rosie.

The next morning I took out my paints and paper. Rosie and Takeo watched me paint.

"We paint too," said Rosie.

Everything the cousins did was
a little bit extra special.

For the last night of the cousins' visit,
I wanted to do something extra special too.

CAMPING
1. Tent
2. Sleeping Bag
3. Flash Lights
4. Friends
5. Snac

"Tonight we are going to camp outside!" I told them.
"No way," said Takeo.
"Too scary," said Rosie.
"It will be so fun," I promised.

"Why don't you camp inside?" said Pop.

I gathered sheets and started to build us a great tent.
Takeo wanted to build his own tent.

"Why don't we just share one tent?" I asked him.

"Brothers and sisters stick together," he said.

Koji was asleep in his crib, so I went to my tent by myself.

I could hear Takeo and Rosie whispering and giggling. I could see their flashlight shining through their tent walls.

My tent was silent and still.

"I'll just go back to my bedroom," I thought. Camping alone was not what I had in mind.

Just then I felt my tent walls rustling. The flashlight shone inside.

"Come on!" Rosie whispered.

Rosie had made a tunnel to connect our tents. I crawled like a silent lion on the prowl, following Rosie's flashlight through the dark tunnel.

The cousins had made a sign for me. It said,
"Firefly Tent, Home of our Best Cousin, Lila."

When the cousins left, we all hugged. Once they were gone, I snuck into our tent. There was a note for me on the pillow.

Dear Lila,
Please come visit our apartment.
Please bring these things:
1. your bike
2. fireflies
3. sheets for the world's biggest tent that we're going to make.
Love your favorite cousins,
Rosie and TAKEO